CHICKEN RUN

CUTTING LOOSE

Behind the Fences at Tweedy's Farm

Written by James Wallis
Designed by Tony Fleetwood

Screenplay by Karey Kirkpatrick
Story by Peter Lord and Nick Park
Directed by Peter Lord and Nick Park
Produced by Peter Lord, David Sproxton and Nick Park

Aardman ™   **DreamWorks** ™   **PATHÉ!** ™

PUFFIN BOOKS

Published by the Penguin Group
Penguin Books Ltd, 27 Wrights Lane, London W8 5TZ, England
Penguin Putnam Books for Young Readers, 345 Hudson Street, New York, New York 10014, USA
Penguin Books Australia Ltd, Ringwood, Victoria, Australia
Penguin Books Canada Ltd, 10 Alcorn Avenue, Toronto, Ontario, Canada M4V 3B2
Penguin Books (NZ) Ltd, 182-190 Wairau Road, Auckland 10, New Zealand

On the World Wide Web at: www.penguinputnam.com

Penguin Books Ltd, Registered Offices: Harmondsworth, Middlesex, England

Published by Puffin Books,
a division of Penguin Putnam Books for Young Readers
1 3 5 7 9 10 8 6 4 2

TM and © 2000 DreamWorks,
Aardman Chicken Run Limited and Pathé Image
Written by James Wallis
Designed by Tony Fleetwood
Screenplay by Karey Kirkpatrick
Story by Peter Lord and Nick Park
Directed by Peter Lord and Nick Park
Produced by Peter Lord, David Sproxton, and Nick Park
All rights reserved

Printed in the United States of America

ISBN 0-14-130878-8

Nick & Fetcher's SCAVENGER SERVICE

Ladies an' gentlemen,

Nick and Fetcher's Scavenger Service is proud to welcome you to the one-and-only official Chicken Run catalogue. We were part of the Chicken Run team and have acquired certain valuable items that we know that you are going to want as souvenirs of this historic event. So, without further ado, Fetcher, the first piece of merchandise, please.

An authentic CHICKEN RUN CHICK—EN EGG! One of Bunty's finest! An' the price of this unique item? We're not asking for riches. All we're asking is ... one egg! ... Hang on a moment, that's not going to work, is it?

PARTY HAT

The fabulous 'Badminton Birdie Hat' as worn by all chic chicks in the fashionable chicken coups of Paris. The only thing to be seen in at this year's barn dance. Price: one egg.

BEAK— WARMER

The latest designer styles in beak wear as knitted by our own fashion guru, Bunty. Price: one egg.

THIS BOOK! And
finally, we move quickly to the last item in our catalogue. This valuable scrapbook! We have assembled this fine souvenir from bits of paper and stuff that came into our possession through various means — mostly ~~we thieved~~ them borrowed them. OK, we'll see you again at the end and if you like it, we'll talk about a price. Can't say fairer than that, can we?

PULLETIN BOARD

THEATRE GROUP
Volunteers needed! The play this year will be Shakesfeather's 'Much Cock-a-Doodle-Do About Nothing'.
Help wanted in all departments.

Sick of chicken-feed? Dolores in Hut 5 hosts '101 New Ways with Worms' Every Saturday night. All welcome.

Would the hen who keeps taking the hay from Hut 12's nests please put it back. The nights are getting cold and so are our bottoms.

Smuggled out of solitary from our mate Ginger.

Dear All,
I'm doing well - only two more days and I'll be out. Don't give up hope! Operation Tightrope may have been a failure (my bruises have almost healed) but we've learned from it. We will escape! We must!
See you soon,
Ginger

MEDITATION AND EGG LAYING.
The natural way to deal with egg stress.
Beginner's class
Thursday,
Hut 12.

BAB'S KNITTING CIRCLE
Meets Hut 2, after Escape Committee meeting. Need suggestions for what to knit when we finish the circle.

ESCAPE COMMITTEE –
TONIGHT, HUT 17,
AFTER LIGHTS-OUT.

Agenda:

1. A minute's silence in memory of Edwina.
2. New plan: ramps and springboards (Mac).
3. Dealing with the dogs: the 'Fetch, Fido!' theory.
4. The Mrs Farmer disguise — it didn't work with the dogs, but would it work with Mr Farmer?
5. Battering ram — where could we get a sheep big enough?

<u>Meeting postponed until Ginger
gets out of solitary</u>

Ladies – need any creature comforts? Nick & Fetcher's Scavenger Service will get them for you.
Very reasonable prices.

Thought for the Day: if this is a chicken farm run by people, does that mean that somewhere there is a people farm run by chickens?

WEEKLY LECTURE –
Mac, on 'Memories of Bonnie Scotland'.
(Translator needed.)

The All-Ladies' Cricket XI
A training session is held every third day, outside Hut 7. Trainer and umpire: Wing Commander Fowler. And if anyone finds our ball, please tell us: it's been lost 4 weeks now and it's difficult to play without it.

MINISTRY OF AGRICULTURE

REPORT ON: Tweedy's Farm, Yorkshire

REASON FOR REPORT: Two anonymous letters received, the first alleging cruelty to chickens, the second simply reading 'they're organized'. Something odd is going on at that farm ...

File number: CRX020
Species: Human

Name: Mrs Melisha Tweedy
Sex: Female

Produces what?:
Eggs – with help from her chickens.

Amount of production:
Not enough, and going down. If she looked after me, I wouldn't lay either.

Distinguishing features:
Blue eyeshadow. Permanent scowl. Lack of feminine charm. Wellington boots.

Temperament:
Fearsomely ambitious and utterly ruthless.

Habits:
Running farm, collecting eggs, shouting at husband, chopping heads off chickens.

Other notes: Mrs Tweedy commented, 'I don't have time to answer any more of your stupid questions, I've got a farm to run and if you lazy bureaucrats ever did any real work instead of wasting taxpayers' money on idiotic surveys, you'd appreciate quite how much time and effort that takes!'

Comments: If she's like this with people, I feel sorry for the poor chickens.

File number: CRX024
Species: Human

Name: Mr Tweedy
Sex: Male

Produces what?:
Aggravation for Mrs Tweedy.

Amount of production:
Far too much, according to Mrs Tweedy.

Distinguishing features:
Bushy eyebrows. Suspicious frown. Wellington boots.

Temperament:
Slow and cunning, but mostly slow.

Habits:
Prowling around the farm late at night with a torch. It's probably so he doesn't have to be in the farmhouse with Mrs Tweedy.

Other notes: Has a ridiculous theory that the chickens are trying to escape.

Comments: Only just cleverer than most of his chickens. No, I take that back. He isn't.

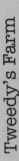
Tweedy's Farm

MINISTRY OF AGRICULTURE

File number: CRX006
Species: Chicken

Name: Ginger
Sex: Female

Produces what?: Eggs.

Amount of production: 1-2 per day.

Distinguishing features: Just your average ginger-coloured chicken wearing a hat and scarf. Nothing special. Quite cute in a chicken kind of a way.

Temperament: Seems pleasant enough, mixes well with others. Mr Tweedy claims that she is the chickens' leader and is organizing them in a massive escape attempt.

Habits: Trying to escape. Relentlessly, to hear Mr Tweedy tell it. Apparently, he's caught her outside the fence five or six times and each time he's shut her in the coal-bunker for a few days 'to teach her a lesson'.

Other notes: My suspicions are confirmed ... there is something very odd going on at Tweedy's Farm.

Comments: Recommend that the farm's security is tightened up, that the Royal Society for the Protection of Chickens is notified about this coal-bunker business, and that Mr Tweedy seeks professional help. As for any reports of mass-escapes by chickens, I think we can safely disregard them.

File number: CRX010
Species: Chicken

Name: Bunty
Sex: Female

Produces what?: Eggs.

Amount of production: Five a day. Yes – five a day.

Distinguishing features: This is a big chicken. There is so much heft to this hen, she may be part ostrich. If turkeys ever go out of fashion, Bunty could take over their job with no trouble at all.

Temperament: I know this section was put on the form for bulls and farmers' wives and other things that can turn nasty so that inspectors like us would know what to beware of, but ... do we really have to include details of a chicken's temperament? She lays eggs. She scratches in the dirt. She eats chicken-feed. She's a chicken. What do you expect?

Habits: Laying eggs, scratching in the dirt, eating chicken-feed, etc.

Other notes: Three-times winner of the All-Yorkshire Champion Egg-Layer trophy. You can see why.

Comments: Bunty's eggs are probably the only thing stopping Tweedy's Farm from falling into bankruptcy.

MINISTRY OF  AGRICULTURE

REPORT ON: Tweedy's Farm, Yorkshire

File number: CRX017
Species: Chicken

Name: Babs
Sex: Female

Produces what?:

Eggs.

Amount of production:

0-1 a day; dropping off, according to Mrs Tweedy.

Distinguishing features:

Inexplicably carries knitting needles with her everywhere, which is unusual for a chicken, particularly one as silly as this. Clucks a lot.

Temperament:

Pleasant, hard-working, but ... this is not the cleverest chicken in the farmyard. It's a wonder she ever worked out how to hatch.

Habits:

See Bunty, but with a bit less egg-laying and a lot more knitting.

Other notes: Reminds me of one of my crazy aunts.

Comments: I wonder ... teaching chickens to knit. It's an unusual idea but could prove very profitable. This could revolutionize the poultry industry.

File number: CRX012
Species: Rooster

Name: Fowler
Sex: Male

Produces what?:

Spluttering noises that sound oddly similar to my Uncle Ed's war stories.

Amount of production:

Quite a lot.

Distinguishing features:

Strange, strutting walk; a crowing noise that sounds like 'Poppycock!'

Temperament:

A tough old bird – emphasis on the 'old' here. In fact, he seems to be showing signs of senility and repetitive behaviour.

Habits:

Strutting. Tries to keep the hens in order. Fails, mostly.

Other notes: A former RAF mascot with 633 Squadron, this cockerel was adopted by the Tweedys when they found out the Air Force wouldn't charge them for taking him away. Has been on the farm ever since.

Comments: May be getting a bit old for the job: the farm would probably be a lot more active if there was a younger male around.

Tweedy's Farm

MINISTRY OF AGRICULTURE

File number: CRX014
Species: Chicken

Name: Mac
Sex: Female

Produces what?: Eggs. And – er – inventions, according to Mr Tweedy.

Amount of production: Eggs: 1 a day. Inventions ... I couldn't find a sign of any.

Distinguishing features: This is the only hen I've ever heard that seems to cluck with a Scottish accent.

Temperament: Well mannered, but basically mad!

Habits: Spends too much time scratching in the dirt (marks that look mysteriously like mathematical formulas) when she should be laying eggs.

Other notes: Mac is too clever to be a hen. She should have been a parrot or a pig because she's useless as a chicken. She may be putting ideas into the other hens' heads, which is not good as most of them don't have room in there for one idea in the first place.

Comments: Clearly a bird of intelligence, but intelligence isn't much use in a chicken. Still, it was nice of her to fix my watch when I dropped it. Hey, wait a moment ...

File number: CRX050
Species: Rats

Name: Nick and Fetcher
Sex: Male

Produces what?: They don't produce things, they 'acquire' them. *Heh, they're on to us!*

Amount of production: Depends how much they're being paid.

Distinguishing features: Squeaking in funny accents; wearing clothes made from old sacks; taking things that aren't theirs.

Temperament: Looking out for their big break; looking out for number one; and looking out for things to steal.

Habits: Stealing things. Daydreaming about eggs.

Other notes: If anyone sees these two, could they get my silver pen back from them?

Comments: Notify Health Department about vermin problem.

Vermin! I'm not having some civil servant calling me vermin!

Dear Diary,

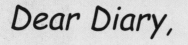

Another day in the coal-bunker dawns dark and dismal. Actually they all dawn like that because the lid's closed.

Life in solitary isn't all bad. There are brief glimpses of the sky when Mr Farmer comes to get some coal, and Nick and Fetcher sneak in to bring me news. The lack of food means that watching my weight is easy and I get plenty of catching practice bouncing this brussel sprout against the wall. But most importantly, it gives me time to think.

What do I think? I think we've got to get out of this farm!

I have to keep strong for the sake of the others. Without me pushing them, the others would be stuck here as firmly as Bunty got stuck under the fence when we tried that digging plan. But chickens are meant to be free, I know it. I've seen it on the side of the boxes they pack our eggs in — 'Free Range'.

This brussel sprout's lost its bounce and its leaves have started coming off. I'll have to ask Nick to bring me another one. Maybe a small turnip would last longer.

The trouble is, we've tried all the obvious plans:
● Digging under the wire.
● Tunnelling.
● Disguising ourselves to get past the guard-dogs.
(I thought the Mrs Farmer outfit was going to work,
although I admit that the back-up plan — trying to dress
up as an attractive female dog — was a mistake.)
● Hiding in the chicken-feeders.
● Tightrope walking across the telephone wires.
● Playing dead (and that was a mistake — poor, poor
Millicent).
    In fact, we've done everything short of making a giant
wooden chicken, hiding in it and hoping that Mr Farmer
will drag it outside the fence. But that's just stupid.
    At least here in solitary — away from Fowler's boring war
stories and Babs talking about knitting and holidays —
I have time to concentrate and think of new ways to escape.
Normally new ideas flood out as fast as eggs from Bunty's
bottom, but this time there's been nothing. And if I can't
come up with anything then we might as well give up and
admit it's over.
        Over ...
        Over the fence ...
        Now that's an idea ...

TWEEDY'S FARM

Melisha Tweedy's Business Plan

EGG YIELD

(graph: Eggs (vertical axis marked 10, 20, 30, 40, 50, 60, 70, 80, 90, 100, 110, 120) vs Month (J F M A M J J A S O N D); line declining over the year)

PROBLEMS

A. Egg yield is down sixty per cent year-on-year.

B. The market price of eggs isn't as safe as it once was.

C. I'm sick to the back teeth of hens and eggs and being stuck out in the
middle of nowhere with nobody but that lump of a husband for company! Things must change.

POSSIBLE SOLUTIONS

1. INCREASE EGG YIELD

✓ How? By doubling the number of chickens? We could cram twice as many in a hut.

✓ Would increase feed costs. But we could cut their rations.

✗ Twice as much clucking. I couldn't stand it.

2. FARM SOMETHING ELSE

✓ Sheep? Too stupid. Pigs? Too smelly. Cows?

✗ We'd have to buy the new animals and find a way to get rid of the chickens.
What could we do with them? Sell them? No, too much work. Think, Melisha, think.

✗ Seaweed! That magazine said there was good money in it. But we'd need to be
near the sea.

3. AUTOMATE PRODUCTION

✓ Very up-to-date and newfangled. We'd be the envy of our neighbours.

✓ I hate all our neighbours.

✗ Machinery is expensive and noisy.

✓ It would drown out the infernal clucking of those horrible birds.

✗ There's nothing to automate that Mr Tweedy can't
do by hand if I bully him enough.

PLAN OF ACTION

Sweet-talk bank manager into extending our overdraft,
using my feminine charm. No, on second thoughts, that
didn't work last time. Bully him into extending our overdraft.

... Oh, this is hopeless. I was a fool to marry that idiot Tweedy.
Thought I could get rich. Well, my big ideas are all just
pie-in-the-sky now. I need to come up with something quick
or I'll be eating humble pie. This should be as easy as pie for a
woman as intelligent as me. Think, Melisha ...

Nick and Fetcher's
Business Plan

Problems

A. Chickens pay us chicken—feed.

B. How are we ever going to join the rat race if we can't earn some decent cash?

C. What we really want is eggs, and loads of 'em.

Possible solutions

1. START PINCHING EGGS

✗ If anything disappears around here, there's only two individuals talented enough to have done it. And that's us. So they'd know.

✗ Chickens spend all their time sitting on their eggs anyway.

✗ We could nick 'em from the farm instead. Mrs Tweedy might catch us ... aarrh! Forget that idea quick.

3. TRY ANOTHER LINE OF BUSINESS

✗ There is no other line of business for us rats.

4. GET THE CHICKENS TO PAY US IN EGGS

✗ Eggs are too valuable to the chickens.

✓ Scavenge stuff the chickens really need.

✓ Chickens have limited lifestyle requirements ... s'pose it can't hurt to ask though.

5. START OUR OWN EGG FARM

✓ Need chickens to lay eggs ... or is it eggs to hatch chickens?

Plan of Action

... what have we decided?

Er... nothing ...

Doing nothing sounds like a good plan.

ESCAPE COMMITTEE

Meeting number: 56   Venue: Hut 17

Chairhen: Ginger   Minutes taken by: Alice

Meeting began as soon as the coast was clear. A minute's silence was observed for poor old Edwina. Ginger called the meeting to order, with the assistance of Fowler. Ginger thanked Fowler. Fowler responded warmly to the thanks and began to tell a story about his RAF days. Ginger thanked him again, and kept thanking him until he shut up.

Ginger reported on recent escape attempts including the disastrous 'whisk' episode that resulted in Ducky receiving a nasty wing injury. Ginger asked the meeting what progress there'd been on escape plans while she'd been in the bunker. The meeting shuffled its feet and didn't say very much, except for Babs who showed everyone her latest knitting project: a scarf for Mac. Everyone clustered round to admire it. Babs said she was pleased by the meeting's reaction and asked if anyone had any more wool – a lot more wool – because she wanted to knit a scarf for Bunty. Ginger objected that this meeting was supposed to be about escaping and Bunty objected that Babs was calling her fat.

Ginger called the meeting back to order and then described a new plan, hatched by her and Mac. Halfway through, Mac took over the explanation and between that and the diagrams she pulled out, I got completely lost. When Mac starts using words like 'tensile strength', 'elasticity quotient' and 'parabola' my brain goes all hurty. When Mac finished the meeting was silent.

$$\frac{13.6}{409 \text{ PSI}} = 27$$

Then Ginger explained it for us. We could escape by putting something like a see-saw next to the fence. A small chicken stands on one end, Bunty jumps on the other, and the small chicken goes up and over the fence.

The meeting wanted to know what would break their fall on the other side. Babs offered to knit something. Further discussion on this point was cut short by Bunty shouting, 'Hold on, you're saying I'm the fattest chicken on the farm'. Mac replied that it wasn't Bunty's size, it was her mass-to-surface-area ratio that mattered. Bunty asked whether Mac was saying her bottom was too big because if she was, then she (Bunty) would take the question further by asking if she (Mac) was looking for a fight.

Ginger interrupted, saying that Bunty would only need to boost one or two small chickens over the fence, because those chickens would take ropes with them to pull the rest up and over the fence from the other side. Fowler wanted to know if that meant we were going to have to pull Bunty over the fence. Mac said she would have to do some maths about whether that was possible, even with every chicken on the farm pulling on the ropes all at once.

The meeting broke up quicker than an old eggshell with everyone shouting at each other; Bunty insisting that she wasn't fat, she was just big-wishboned; Mac saying she was sorry but, darn it, hen, she was a scientist not an agony aunt. I saw Ginger go outside to sit on the roof, where she usually goes when she wants to be alone and think about things. So, just a typical Escape Committee meeting really.

$$A + B = C$$
$$\frac{M^2}{100}$$
$$5\text{kg} = \frac{X + Y}{90}$$

MAC'S ESCAPE PLAN No. 24

So, Bunty won't go for my fulcrum-principle idea. Och well. There's plenty more great plans where that came from.

The 'Over-the-Fence' Theory –
Ginger thinks going over the wire is the way forward. She may have something. But if we can't use Bunty's mass as the power-source, then we need something else. We could try the old one-two-heave-ho and a leg-up. But that's no' scientific! We need to know how much potential energy there is in a heave-ho and how much in a leg-up or we'll have hens crashing into the fence or getting caught in the barbed wire at the top. Mind, a heave-ho from Bunty would most likely put you up next to that Sputnik.

$$22\sqrt{345°}$$
$$E$$

The Spring Theory –
A big coil o' wire, and the hen hits it at X mph, – where X is a number higher than the mass x the escape-velocity in foot-pounds squared, – whereby the kinetic energy is transferred into vertical thrust, and ... But it would take a big spring – and very fast chickens.
Or ... no. That's just stupid.

$$5kg = \frac{X+Y}{90}$$

$$X = Y^3$$

The Pole Theory –
But, if we took the spring and straightened it out into a pole, and a hen ran at the wire with it and dug one end o' the pole into the ground at the bottom of the fence ... then with conservation o' momentum and a spring in her step, she'd go up with the other end o' the pole. And if she let go at the right moment, she'd be over the top and away! And the pole would fall back for the next hen. Mac, you're a genius!

$$\frac{a+B}{M^2}{100}$$

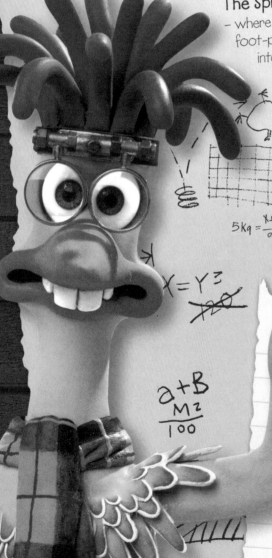

ESCAPE REPORT

Nick and Fetcher got us a pole. Ginger volunteered. Everything seemed to be going well – Ginger ran at the fence and up she goes on the end o' the pole. One o' the dogs sees something's amiss and comes bounding over. Ginger realises that if she lets go she'll fly over the wire and land on top of the dog. Sensible hen doesn't let go – but loses her grip and slides down the pole into the barbed wire. Ouch! The dog barks. Mr Farmer sees Ginger caught in the wire. Four days in the coal-bunker for Ginger. Back to the drawing board for me.

PULLETIN BOARD

STOP PRESS: We have a very special visitor all the way from America. Rocky Rhodes the flying rooster.

Learn to Fly

Third lesson begins tomorrow morning. Subjects will include basic flapping and some advanced flapping, if Rocky thinks we're up to it. Come on, ladies, you're all doing really well. We'll be flying over that fence to freedom very soon – you'll see!

Nick an' Fetcher's Scavenger Service is proud to announce these new items in its range of chicken-care products:
FLY-PAPER To give you some of that extra lift which none of you 'ave mastered yet.
MASSAGE OIL Ease those tired feathers with the stylish and exclusive 'Moto-Lube' brand, as worn by all the best-dressed humans.
AN' FOR ANY NON-CHICKENS Buy a seat on Nick an' Fetcher's grandstand to watch these bird-brains trying to fly. Laugh? We thought we'd never stop.

WEEKLY LECTURE –

Our American visitor, Rocky Rhodes, will give a talk on his life and travels. There is a limit on space, so arrive early.

Can we ask questions?

Will he be wearing the scarf I made him?

Can I have a signed photo?

~~WEEKLY LECTURE~~ Next Week's Lecture

will be by Wing Commander Fowler, on 'How We Won the Battle of Britain With No Help From Anyone Else'.

Someone has been taking hay from Hut 8. Please put it back. Our eggs are rolling out of our nests and getting mixed up. Hut 12? Is that you? Stop it!

All the way from the US of A – BASEBALL starts tonight outside Hut 7. If anyone finds the cricket ball, can we borrow it? Or if not, a small turnip or brussel sprout?

Found the ball! Millicent in Hut 19 was trying to hatch it!

Colonel Daniel Spoon Presents

TRAVELLING CIRCUS

SEE the world's smallest elephant!

WITNESS the tamest lion in captivity!

GASP at the world's most terrifying clowns!

★★★★★★★★ Be amazed by ★★★★★★★★

GUNTAR THE KNIFE THROWER

★★★★★★ and his assistant *Sabrina* ★★★★★★

You'll never forget **LUCINDA** and her feats on **EUROPE'S SHORTEST TIGHTROPE**

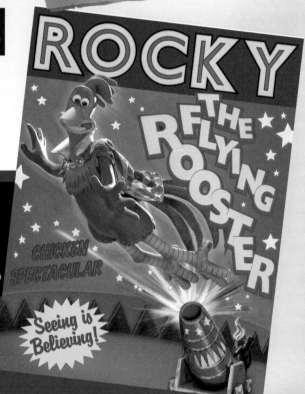

ROCKY THE FLYING ROOSTER

CHICKEN SPECTACULAR

Seeing is Believing!

AND OUR GRAND STAR...

All the way from the USA...
The original
Kentucky Flying Chicken

TURN YOUR CHICKEN FARM INTO A GOLDMINE

Quality

Farmers! Are you looking for a way to make your flock pay? Do you yearn to earn more than chicken-feed? If you've got chickens, Poultry Products Ltd has the answer to your dreams. You'll use every part of the chicken except the cluck.

A family-owned business, Poultry Products Ltd has been making pies and meat-processing equipment for over one hundred years. Now, ready for the technological demands of the modern age and the boom in pre-packaged frozen foods, we present the Pie Machine range. The Pie Machine – it does the work while you have a cup of tea!

Model 100 – Our introductory model can produce a pie (uncooked) every five minutes. Requires chickens to be plucked, gutted and de-boned and pastry to be pre-mixed. Only vegetable currently available is potato. Model 100 is suitable for small farms, those on a budget, or those making low-quality pies to be sold cheap.

Model 200 – The basic pie-creating workhorse, Model 200 transforms a plucked chicken into a succulent nine-inch pie, including modules for de-boning, meat-grinding and crust-stuffing.

Model 500X – Top of the range, running at up to 6ppm (pies per minute). Able to handle different sizes of birds and creates pies from three to twelve inches. You can configure everything, from the meat-to-veg mix ratios, to how finely the chicken-meat is chopped (including extra grinders for tougher old birds). Includes circular auto-sharpening knives, vegetable slicers, dough mixers, our patented 'Skwirtt' gravy-adding system and plenty of exciting buttons, dials and blinking lights to impress your neighbours. Winner of the Gold Medal last year at the Congres dés Poules in Paris.

'Whenever I start up my Model 200 Pie Machine, my neighbours lean out of their windows across the valley and wave their arms at me. They're envious, I can tell.'
– B. M., Shropshire

All prices on application. Easy payment terms. One hundred per cent deposit required before delivery. Delivery within a week of order. Some assembly required. Chickens not included.
Write for further information to: Poultry Products Ltd (prop. George Lovett), Fleet Street, London EC4 8JB

My Life &

Rocky: My, my, what a turnout – thanks for coming, girls, it's really great to see you all here. I'm getting to be quite the celebrity around these parts, right? So you want to know all about me? Well, I'll start right at the beginning for you. I was laid and hatched in the great American state of Kentucky.

Babs: Hen-tucky?

Rocky: Ken-tucky, Babs. Anyway, as I was saying ...

Babs: What's Kentucky like?

Fowler: Ken Tucky – didn't he play cricket for Somerset before the war?

Rocky: What's Kentucky like? Well, it's big, and it's far away, and it doesn't rain so much.

All the hens: Ooooo.

Rocky: My ma – she was the greatest. So when her birthday rolled around, I thought, well, Rocky, you've got a pretty swell voice, why don't you give her a song? So I started to practise a little number called 'Love me tender' – I'd seen a poster about tender chickens, so I thought she'd like it. So anyway, I'm singing and the next thing I know I'm picked up and carried away by the farmer. He sells me to this guy named Colonel

Spoon. The Colonel didn't have a musical career in mind for me – he was keen to exploit my other talent.

Babs: Oooo you like knitting too?

Rocky: No Babs. I mean my talent for flying. Didn't even know I could do it before the Colonel ... er ... encouraged me to try.

Fowler: You flew? Just like that?

Rocky: Yep, like a missile. I'm a natural.

Fowler: Poppycock! Nobody goes solo their first time. In my RAF days it took months to train a pilot.

Rocky: Well, believe it or not, pops, I flew. My first landing wasn't great – I hit an elephant – but I survived. Overnight I became the Colonel's star attraction and, well, add in one trip across the ocean and the rest is history. Here I am, teaching you sweet chicks all I know. Any questions?

Fowler: So why did you crash into our farmyard?

Rocky: Oh, I, er ... I was working on a tricky new stunt and got caught in a tail-wind.

Fowler: Poppycock!

Dear Diary,

Something's going wrong. When Rocky first arrived I thought he was the answer to all my prayers. He's only been here a few days, but already I'm beginning to wonder. I'm no expert on flying, but I've watched mother birds teaching their chicks how to fly, and none of it has involved press-ups, jumping jacks and skipping. And now Mac says that according to her calculations, chickens can't fly without 'throost'. I know as little about calculations as I do about flying, but I trust Mac a lot more than I trust Rocky.

But he can fly. And if he can then we can. Maybe I'm just doubting myself. If only his wing would heal and he could show us how to fly this coop, instead of giving us PE lessons.

I sent Nick and Fetcher to see if they could find anything in the farmhouse that would help Rocky's wing to heal. The only thing they brought back was a page from a book they'd seen in the kitchen, that said 'How to Fix Chicken Wings'. I read on, but it was a page from a cookery book and oh my goodness, the horror! The horror! I felt quite faint after reading it.

Rocky's been quite a hit with the other hens. They'd do anything for him and he knows it, and I think he's enjoying it a little too much. Still, you can't blame them when the only cockerel they've had to look at before is Fowler. Fowler doesn't trust Rocky — doesn't like Americans at all it seems. Mind you, I don't trust any rooster, Fowler included.

I'm not like the other hens though — I won't fall prey to Rocky's American charm — if you can call it charm. Doll-face, humph! But I think I will go and see how his talk is going. Just to keep an eye on the others, mind. Not because I'm interested ...

Ginger

Mrs Tweedy's Marketing Plans
Pie-Boxes and Labels

● WHAT DO WE CALL THEM?

~~Tweedy's Farm Pies~~

~~Mrs Tweedy's Chicken Pies~~

Mrs Tweedy's Home-Made Chicken Pies

Mrs Tweedy's Delicious Home-Made Chicken Pies

~~Mrs Tweedy's Really Amazingly Delicious Home-Made Chicken Pies~~

Mrs Tweedy's Best Chicken Pies in the World, Ever, Ever, Ever, Ever.

... Needs more work.

● SLOGANS

~~Like your mother used to make~~ *Like your bossy older sister used to make*

Like your mother would have made if she was as good a cook as Mrs Tweedy

Better than the pies that awful Vera Rushton makes

~~As fresh as the moment the chicken went 'cluck, AARGH!'~~

If it's not Tweedy, it's weedy'

● INGREDIENTS' LIST

Fresh chicken, best pastry, fresh vegetables, delicious gravy, salt, pepper, artificial colours, artificial flavourings, artificial preservatives and artificial flavour-enhancers.

Best not to mention artificial ingredients at all.

Who's going to check?

● WEIGHT

Can this include the pie-tin and box?

● BEST BEFORE

Just put a day and a month, but no year.
If any get sent back, we'll store 'em for a
few months and send 'em back out.

Quality

Best label for package

Daily Dales Reporter

No. 1154   Price: Tuppence ha'penny

PIE MACHINE LEADS TO BOOM

Automation threat to local way of life?

Tweedy's Farm, which has produced chickens for generations, is set to become the centre of a boom in the local economy. On Tuesday the owners, Mr and Mrs Tweedy, took delivery of the latest model 500X Pie Machine from London, which is able to produce up to six oven-ready chicken pies per minute.

As the key part of an ambitious plan to sell pies across the country, the pie machine will transform the farm's traditional way of life into a chicken-processing frenzy.

Job Boom

It is understood that the Tweedys are considering employing a part-time helper to add the vegetables, pastry and gravy to the machine and to carry the boxed pies. This will have a major impact on local unemployment figures.

'We may be thinking about hiring someone,' said Mrs Melisha Tweedy, whose name and picture will appear on the pie-boxes. 'After all, when the business takes off we'll be rich and you can't expect rich people to do dirty work like bending and carrying. We wouldn't be paying much though.'

'Chickens go in, pies come out,' added Mr Tweedy, who is in charge of the machine's assembly and maintenance.

The Tweedys are understood to be the envy of their neighbours.

Threat to Life

The move has not been entirely popular. 'This machine threatens our way of life: the great Yorkshire tradition of making chicken pies by hand,' said Mrs Vera Rushton, whose pies won a prize at last year's local village show. 'I don't want to eat something made by an awful machine that might have dripped screws or oil into it.'

Mrs Tweedy was quick to respond: 'I've eaten one of Mrs Rushton's pies,' she said, 'and not only was it nasty, I found a hair in it. Our pies will not have hairs in them. That's the benefit of modern living, but people like her won't move with the times.'

'Chickens go in, pies come out,' added Mr Tweedy again.

Mr and Mrs Tweedy, local technological pioneers

CHICKEN STILL ON RUN

Rocky, the amazing flying chicken who escaped from Colonel Daniel Spoon's circus several days ago, has still not been caught, despite a five-guinea reward.

The American rooster disappeared in a puff of smoke when the cannon from which he was launched every night was accidentally given a double-charge of gunpowder, and he was last seen heading north-west at high speed.

HIGH POINT

Rocky's daring act thrilled local people recently when Colonel Spoon's circus came to town. His stunt closed the show and, as our critic (Sandra Lee, aged 7) commented at the time, was the high point of an otherwise lacklustre show, although the ponies and the orange drink were nice.

'Rocky is our star,' said Colonel Spoon, 'and his value is beyond rubies. If he isn't found I will be making a large claim on my insurance. Can you mention we'll be back in town same time next year?'

NO DANGER

Members of the public should be reassured that apart from his ability to fly, Rocky is a completely normal rooster and poses no danger to anyone who finds him. He is not related to Feathers McGraw, the notorious jewel thief who was in the news recently, who wears a cunning chicken disguise.

On other pages: This week's recipe: Duck à L'Orange Squash, p.7. Reader's letter, p.10. Cross word: botheration. Adverts for pig-feed and tractors, p.11-27. Cricket, p. 28.

Tweedy's Farm
The Dales,
Yorkshire
YD3 6HD

Dear Doctor Jones,

I'm writing to you because I have a serious personal problem that won't go away. My husband.

For the last few weeks, Mr Tweedy has become obsessed with the idea that the chickens on our farm are plotting behind his back. It all started when he found one (a scruffy little ginger item who I admit's been nothing but trouble) outside the fence. Since then, he's claimed that he's caught the chickens tunnelling out of the farm, sneaking out hidden in feeders, doing press-ups, and even trying to escape disguised as me.

This is a very important time for the farm and I need Mr Tweedy to be working as hard as he can, not wasting his energy worrying about some daft idea of escaping chickens. I know he's not going mad because he's much too stupid, but all this chicken-talk is cutting into his work time, and I cannot tolerate that.

Is there some sort of pill I could give Mr Tweedy so he'll calm down, shut up and do what he's told? And is it available on the National Health, so I don't have to pay?

Yours sincerely,

Melisha Tweedy

Doctor H. Jones
The Surgery, Baxendale, Yorkshire

Dear Mrs Tweedy,

Thank you for your letter. I recommend you tell your husband to pull himself together and stop acting like a blithering idiot. Failing that, get rid of him. If getting rid of him is not an option, give him two aspirins and call me in a week if he's not better.

Looking forward to trying one of your pies.

Sincerely,

ROCKY'S GUIDE TO LIFE

Part One: Flying

Flying. Lemme tell you, flying is just about the greatest thing there is and once you know how, it's about as easy as falling off a bridge.

OK now, if you're gonna fly then there are seven things you need. We've been through the big three already: hard work, perseverance and more hard work; and you chicks are doing great at them. But there's four more and they're just as important.

ATTITUDE means that the biggest thing in flying ain't your wings or your legs, it's your state of mind. You gotta think like a flyer. Pull yourself up, stick your chest out, flap your wings and say, 'I can fly. I'm a flyer. I'm a chicken. I feel light. I feel like a chicken who's light.' If you can't remember all of it, just work with the last bit: 'I feel like a chicken who's light – a chicken who's light.' Catchy, isn't it? Keep repeating it until you believe it and keep flapping your wings. It may sound weird, but trust me, in a few years everyone'll be doing it.

ALTITUDE Start from somewhere high up, like a chair or a box or a tall building. Because I'm going to let you in on a big secret here: the quickest way to learn to fly is to jump off something and remember not to fall.

RHYTHM All the great flyers got rhythm. You ever hear the saying 'they heard the beating of wings'? Well, wings gotta have a beat or they don't work right! You're in luck because I'm from the USA, and the USA is where beat was invented.

THRUST Thrust is oomph, it's power, it's get-up-and-go. You gotta have thrust, and thanks to Mr Tweedy's braces that Nick and Fetcher so kindly acquired for us, we do. So you girls keep with the flapping practice while Mac rigs up one of her inventions to help you all get airborne, and I – I think I'll sit in the shade and watch you. Gotta be careful with this wing, you know.

The Public Speaks Its Mind

We ask ordinary members of the public about a burning issue of the day. Today's question is:

'WHAT DO YOU THINK ABOUT CHICKENS LEARNING TO FLY?'

Nick, entrepreneur
'I think it's great! Watching them chickens lyin' on trolleys and catapultin' themselves into the fence today was the funniest thing I saw since ... well, since yesterday.'

Fetcher, enternp – I mean entrereper – I sell stuff
'Yeah, what Nick said. But chickens flyin'? It ain't normal and it ain't proper – against nature, it is. Chickens should stick to chicken stuff, and rats like us'll stick to what we do – which is 'nickin' and 'fetchin', mostly.'

Anonymous chicken, egg-layer
'I'm not sure about this whole flying thing. It seems like a lot of silly fuss to me, and for what? To get out of here, where they house us and feed us and give us somewhere to live, and all we have to do for them is keep laying eggs? I'm telling you, I wouldn't be bothering with it if it weren't for that Rocky. Ooh, I think he's lovely. And if flying's good enough for him then it's good enough for the likes of me, I reckon.'

Gnome (wouldn't give name)
Preferred to stay silent on the subject.

Bonzo, guard dog
'GRRRrrrrr.'
'Is that an expression of disapproval, Mr Bonzo?'
'RrrrrrrrrrrRRRRRRrrr.'
'Yes, well, thank you for your time but we must be – Ow! AARGH!'

Mr Tweedy, farmer
'It's all in me head, it's all in me head, it's all in me head, she says it's all in me head so it must be all in me head.'

Fowler, former RAF Wing Commander
'I've got just one thing to say on the subject of cocky know-it-all jumped-up Americans coming over here and eyeing up our womenfowl under the pretence of teaching them to fly, which is a damn-fool notion if ever I heard one, and acting like idiots in an attempt to sway their silly young minds – and that's, no comment.'

How we won the BATTLE OF BRITAIN without any help from the Americans

Fowler: I don't think anyone else is going to come so shall we start? Thank you all for coming ... all four of you. I'm very pleased to have been asked here tonight by the chairhen ... who seems mysteriously absent, probably called away on urgent business ... to tell you the story of the Battle of Britain, in which I played an important part. As Chipper Minton used to say in the officers' mess, a good story can't be told often enough, and this particular story has a timely moral to it. It's about Americans, and the fact that you can't trust 'em.

It was the beginning of World War Two and old Blighty stood alone ... Aah, good old Blighty, this sceptered isle, this seat of Mars, this other Eden, this precious stone set in the silver sea ...

Ducky: He's talking nonsense. I've had enough of this. I'm off.

Fowler: ... but I digress, back to the American's. Well, there weren't any Americans! It took them a couple of years and someone sinking half their navy to notice the rest of the world was having a bit of a war! You can't depend on them when it matters! That's my point, you silly hens!

Ethel: What! I'm not staying here to be insulted.

Agnes: Hold up, Ethel, I'm coming with you. Let's see what Rocky and the others are doing.

Fowler: No, don't go! This is important! You've got to understand that you shouldn't trust ... Oh, what's the point? He's got you under his spell already. But I came here to tell you about the Battle of Britain, and by golly I will. Where was I? Ah, yes, the battle. I was with the Poultry Division attached to 633 Squadron. There were four of us boys and the four lead aircraft all had call-signs named after us. Since we were the four call-sign birds, back at base there were three French hens, which was someone's idea of a joke. One of them was called Marie.

I used to carry one of her feathers with me each time we went out on a bombing run. She had the sweetest beak... but back on track, Fowler old chap. Something was afoot; the word came through and we were in the air in a minute. Suddenly there they were: enemy planes. Hundreds of them coming in over the Channel to give Blighty a pasting. Well, we opened up on 'em with everything we had and eventually we saw them off.

As soon as we touched down and debriefed I went to find Marie, but she wasn't there. She had been killed, you see, in that first wave of bombing. I still have her feather, you know.

And that's why you should be wary of Americans. They may say they're the defenders of freedom and liberty, but when things get rough you can't trust them to help or even to be there. And I hope it's a lesson you'll take to heart, you who are still here ... is anyone still here? I can't see to the back, my eyes aren't what they were ...

Babs: I'm here. When are we going to start?

Fowler: Start? Start what?

Babs: Knitting. This is the knitting circle, isn't it?

Fowler: Hut 2, Babs. Knitting is in Hut 2. Oh dear ...

ROCKY'S GUIDE TO LIFE

Part Two: Chicks

Chicks. What can I say? When it comes to knowing how to deal with the fine feathered female of the species, your pal the Rockster is rooster numero uno.

'Course, English chicks aren't like American ones. Different ways of behaving, different ways of doing things, different ideas about presents to give a guy (a beak-warmer? I love it!) But a chick's a chick, whatever her accent or the colour of her feathers.

But I'm not a love-'em-leave-'em kind a guy. I mean, the crazy English chicks may have flipped over me, but I'm not the sort who swoops too soon. I could be layin' the old romantic deal on any one of them — that Babs is just nuts for me ... or maybe she's just nuts. But I know what I like in a chick — she has to be strong of character and fine of feather, and I'm quite partial to Ginger's feathers ... I mean ginger feathers.

Er ... where was I? Ah, yes, whether you've got your beady eye on one swell hen or if you're just lookin' to make a hit with the birds generally, you'll still need a helping wing. Because if there's one thing all guys have in common, it's that we can't understand what makes the womenflock cluck. Well, with Rocky's guide to chicks that doesn't matter! All you gotta do is remember these four points:

THREADS If you wanna be the centre of attention, you gotta think about what you wear says about you. Take me. I wear this old blue neck-scarf because it shows I'm independent, I'm a lone free ranger. Mac's tartan scarf shows she's Scottish, Bab's beads are ... well, they're like her beady eyes. So threads don't just say who you are, they tell you about the chick that's wearing them. Learn to read them.

ATTITUDE Attitude is what you need to make doll face ... I mean chicks fall at your feet. They gotta think that you're offerin' something they can't find any place else: some escape from that lonely old roof she sits on dreaming of freedom ... did I just say that out loud? Skip it. Now, OK, for me it's easy; I'm a good-lookin' American rooster, the only male in a farm fulla females — not countin' that relic Fowler and trust me, he don't count — and they think I can teach 'em how to fly out. The trick is to let them think what they want. Flatter them in little ways, but never open up and tell 'em your secrets or you're sunk — in the nearest pond.

MOVES You gotta have the moves down. The way you walk, the way you stand, all of that stuff will turn a hen's head too. And most important, you gotta know how to dance. And I'm not talkin' about any of that waltzy-waltzy or hokey-cokey baloney, OK? I'm talkin' rock n roll, the only kinda music that really lets you shake your tailfeather. So, just follow ol' Rocky's step-by-step guide to rock n roll ... step-by-step, you get it?

Step One

Step Two

GETAWAY ROUTE When I say you need a getaway route, I mean you need two. You gotta be able to get away in person and you also gotta know how to put the chick at the back of your mind. The second part ... well, pal, you'll have to work that out for yourself because I seem to be having a little difficulty with this one lately. But don't tell anyone, OK? 'Love 'em, leave 'em and then come back to 'em' — it sounds a bit ... well, a bit chicken, if you know what I mean.

Pie Machine Model 500X

Dos and Don'ts

The Model 500X Pie Machine is a machine so simple that it can be operated by a complete idiot. However, even if you are a complete idiot there are still some important guidelines you must follow. In particular, please note the following points or you may invalidate your guarantee:

DO NOT assemble or service the Model 500X yourself to save money.

DO NOT insert live chickens into the Model 500X. Are you some kind of monster?

DO NOT allow unrestrained live chickens to rampage around inside the Model 500X. This may damage the machine and affect the quality of your pies – see below.

DO NOT place any objects in the gravy hopper that could block the flow (e.g. vegetables, loose packaging, farm dogs, etc).

DO NOT use the Model 500X to make pies other than chicken by placing other pie ingredients (e.g. apples, steaks, kidneys, shepherds, cottages, farm dogs etc.) in the machine.

DO carefully monitor all gauges and indicators on the Model 500X control panel while the machine is in operation and stop the machine immediately if any of them goes into the red zone.

If you must allow an idiot to operate the machine please make sure there is a proper grown-up present at all times.

If you have any problems with your Model 500X Pie Machine, DO NOT attempt to fix it yourself. Shut down the machine and call an authorized engineer. Failure to do so may result in damage to the mechanism of your machine, under- or over-cooking of pies, enormous farmhouse-obliterating explosions of gravy, pastry and vegetables, some very startled farm-dogs, and the invalidation of your guarantee.

What to Do If Live Chickens Are Rampaging around inside Your Model 500X Pie Machine

DO
1. Press the big button that says 'off'.
2. Telephone to arrange a visit by a
Poultry Products Ltd engineer.
3. Put the kettle on and make a cup of tea.

DO NOT
1. Flip every lever in sight without any idea
what you're doing. This is very important, even if you are a complete idiot.
2. Go into the machine yourself to catch the chickens (small farmers only).
3. Allow the chickens to get out of the machine and warn the others that they're going to be
made into pies – ha ha, just our little joke. Of course, chickens aren't clever enough for that.

MAC'S ESCAPE PLAN No. 25

Everyone's caught up in the flying lessons with yon Rocky, but I've been thinking about all this talk o' throost. We never had a chance to test Ginger's idea of going o'er the wire with a catapult. Now we've got Mr Tweedy's trouser braces that the rats brought and I can see the mistakes we made from the calculations I've been doing.

Mistake 1: If you're testing flying ideas, it's a bad idea to use a big hen like Bunty.

Mistake 2: We should have started from somewhere high up.

Mistake 3: We used Bunty.

Mistake 4: We failed to factor in wind speed, direction, barometric pressure and relative humidity.

So forget the horizontal launch, which means the hen has to use her wings for all o' the lift to get over the fence. Instead, launch at an angle (optimum trajectory = mass of hen x height of fence factored by the cosine o' throost-strength, no' forgetting to add a margin of error and one for the pot) so it's the throost that gets them o'er. And they can glide down using their wings. Brilliant!

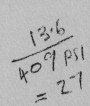

$$\frac{13.6}{409 \text{ PSI}} = 27$$

$$5 \text{ kg} = \frac{x+y}{99}$$

$$\frac{22}{\sqrt{245}}°\ E$$

ESCAPE REPORT

After what happened to the turnip we used for the catapult tests, I thought maybe we shouldn't try this one with a real hen. So I built a decoy hen with a bit o' the dress we used for the Mrs Farmer plan stuffed with hay. I rigged up the catapult at the back of Hut 17, calculated the wind speed, cranked it up and let fly.

Oh, it was beautiful. A perfect parabola, exactly to my calculations.

One snag though: the dress caught on the barbed wire and ripped. One o' the dogs jumped for it as it came down, and it exploded o'er him, bits of hay everywhere. When it cleared there was a dog in a dress with golden straw for hair. He looked lovely. Best of all, nobody was sent to the bunker. A success!

Exploding decoy hens ... that gives me an idea ...

PULLETIN BOARD

STOP PRESS

Rocky has gone. He was a fraud from a circus. He wasn't so much a flying rooster as a lying rooster. Everything's back to normal.
And – I'm so sorry.

I'm not one to blow my own wattles, but I do recall saying that Rocky Rhodes wasn't all he claimed, and although I take no satisfaction in being proved right, I *Oh, stop crowing Fowler.*

Don't worry everyone. Maybe Rocky's just gone on holiday, like Ginger used to, and he'll be back soon. That's what I reckon.

Shut up, Babs.

Two fully trained massage assistants, recently lost jobs due to drop in demand, seek other employment. Offers to Maureen and Gertrude in Hut 11.

DANCING LESSONS
Outside Hut 7, every other evening after flying practice. CANCELLED.

DUE TO CANCELLATION of large order, we've SLASHED PRICES on FINE BEAUTY SUPPLIES, as provided by Mrs Farmer herself.
On offer:
● Blue eyeshadow. 1 seed each.
● Scent, Eau de Vache (That's French that is) come and take it away, cos we reckon it stinks.

FOR SALE: Long lease on purpose-built grandstand overlooking former flight-training grounds. Some damage where Bunty crashed into it. Would suit very small hen. Price: two eggs. Apply: Nick & Fetcher.

The Knitting Circle is making a ~~cape for Rocky~~
If anyone knows how to turn a half-finished cape into something nice and British, come to the Knitting Circle.

RIGHT EVERYONE,
WE'VE GOT A NEW PLAN.
ESCAPE COMMITTEE, HUT 17,
HALF AN HOUR.
NO ABSENTEES!
NO EXCUSES!

Dear Diary,

We've pulled victory from the jaws of the farm dogs ... or have we? I can't tell you how low everyone was after they learned that Rocky had gone. I really thought he cared and I trusted him.

Oh, don't blame yourself. The others went along with it and it was fun while it lasted. And that dance. I've never felt anything like it. And the way he rescued me from that horrid machine ... actually, it was more me rescuing him in the end, but it's the thought that counts. So it's more than disappointment I'm feeling, it's something else as well. I'm not sure what to call it.

But no time for that! Suddenly, after years of listening to the old bird blustering on, we finally found out what Fowler's precious RAF' stands for – and it's not 'Rubbish-talking Aged Fowl', as I'd always thought – and now we have a completely new escape plan. We are going to fly out of here, without that fraud Rocky!

Mac's on the other side of the hut, working on the blueprints (I wish Nick and Fetcher had been able to get us a different colour of paper) for what we're calling the Flying Machine. Not a particularly inventive name I know, but the only other suggestions were Babs': The Big Wooden Thing What We Built', and 'The Old Crate, Mark 2', which was Fowler's. Meanwhile, the rats are off scavenging; Bunty's laying eggs like a ... like a ... there isn't anything like Bunty laying eggs; and Babs is knitting of course.

All of us are going as fast as we can because we're all just waiting to hear the sound of that terrible machine starting up again. That would mean just one thing: we'd failed. I don't think I could escape from it again, not without Rocky's help – why can't I get that bird out of my brain?

But if everyone keeps working together and if Mac can come up with a design that works, and if we can build it and if Fowler can fly it, then we'll be free! It's a lot of ifs, but I've got to trust in the others.

We're so nearly on our way to that green hill, I can taste it ... and it tastes so much better than chicken-feed. Oh, I can't wait. If only Rocky could be here now ... I mean, see us now.

Ginger

Nick and Fetcher's Guide to Scavenging

SCAVENGER SERVICE

LESSON ONE: HAMMERS

You will need: stealth, perfect timing, a faithful companion – and a big gormless bloke with a hammer.

DO sneak up unseen on the gormless bloke.

DO wait, using your perfect timing, for him to put the hammer down.

DO grab the hammer with your faithful companion's help and leg it.

DO NOT drop the hammer on your foot.

LESSON TWO: SPANNERS

You will need: string, agility, daring, a faithful companion who can tie knots and a big gormless bloke with a spanner. Or just a spanner.

DO tie one end of string to roof-beam.

DO wait for the gormless bloke to put the spanner on his workbench.

DO swing your faithful companion on the string over to the bench.

DO tie the string to the spanner and swing back with it.

DO NOT tie your tail to the string by accident, so you swing back upside down looking like a complete idiot.

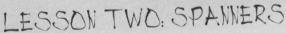

LESSON THREE: SCREWDRIVERS

You will need: a disguise, stealth, cunning, a faithful companion, a gormless bloke with a screwdriver and a diet plan.

DO put on your disguise. Something like a garden gnome.

DO sneak up on the gormless bloke and wait for him to put the screwdriver down.

DO grab the screwdriver and leg it.

And whatever you do, DO make sure you're not so fat that you get stuck inside the garden gnome and have to have your faithful pal use the hammer from Lesson One to smash it to get you out.

PULLETIN BOARD

Escape Committee: Staff Rota

Mac – Engineering
Fowler – Chief Aviation Advisor
Babs – Manufacturing
Ducky – Security
Agnes – Diversions
Nick and Fetcher – Acquisitions *Wot?*
Bunty – Eggs *Pinching stuff, mate*
Ginger – Team Leader

Right everyone, we've got to pull together! We don't have long before Mr Farmer mends that machine and everybody has to do their bit.
So no slacking.

~~Knitting Circle~~ Manufacturing

I've got a list of what we need to make. Here goes:

What part	Who makes it	What out of
Bodywork	Dora	Wool
Wings	Edna	Wool
Tailplane	Alice	Wool
Steel wires	Noreen	Wool
Wooden frame	Babs (me)	Wool

Babs – before your girls start their knitting, could we have a wee chat? – Mac

Acquisitions.

Nick an' Fetcher at your service. Just tell us what you need and we'll get it. One egg per item.

Diversions Committee

Ways to divert and confuse the dogs:
1. Pretend to be mad.
2. Bark at them.
3. Throw the cricket ball for them to fetch.
4. Wait until they're asleep, then throw chicken-feed at them. When they wake up, tell them it was the other dog.

Other ideas to the Diversions Committee, please.

Security Squad

For your security and safety, the following instructions will be obeyed at all times:
1. A complete black-out during the hours of darkness. No clucking after lights-out. This is for your own safety.
2. Obey all instructions immediately and without question. This is for your own protection.
3. Watch your fellow hens for suspicious behaviour and report anything unusual to Security Chief Ducky. This is for your own good.

Here's today's official Morale Committee joke to keep your spirits up.
Knock knock.
Who's there?
Butterfly.
Butterfly who?
Butterfly out of here soon or we'll all be turned into pies.

The Egg Committee wants to know if anyone's got any ointment for her bottom, which is getting sore with all this laying.

MAC'S ESCAPE PLAN No. 26

The Flying Machine

'We'll fly out in a crate,' Ginger says. 'Mac'll design it,' Ginger says. No' a hint of 'please' or 'Mac, is it technically possible to design an aerodynamically stable crate that'll generate enough lift and speed to carry its own weight plus all the chickens on the farm, and could you whip one up before supper?' And I'm tellin' ye straight – I'm no' sure it can be done. Still, better wait until I've done all the calculations.

Materials

Whatever we can get. Which will mostly be wood, wool and chicken feed. Because it always is.

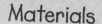

AXLE

2-WHEELS GOOD

Power – What to Use?

First best: Would be the motor from yon pie machine, but the farmer might notice it was gone. And I'm not sure those two rats could lift it.

Second best: Mr Farmer's braces, wound up like a big rubber-band. But even if they can stand his massive stomach, I'm not sure they could stand the pressure we'd need.

Third best: Chicken power. No extra fuel needed. But not as reliable as real engines, 'specially if Babs starts gassin' or knittin' halfway through take-off.

Question: If one chicken can't get itself into the air, how are we going to get this contraption full of chickens to fly? We need more efficient power-to-weight ratios. More aerodynamic wings. Proper propellers? Flapping or not? What's the best gearing to use for the power-transmission system? Come on, Mac, this is the greatest challenge you've ever faced. You can do it!

Take-Off

No' much room for a runway. I was thinking of a vertical take-off, but I cannae see a way of doing it wi'out making it a vertical landing too – straight up, straight down, land in a big heap on the spot you took off from. We'll just have to hope for a good pilot and the right wind. And as Fowler's the pilot, the wind'll have to be very right indeed. Feathers crossed.

NOSE

DOUBLE-STRENGTH STITCHING

COCKPIT

BABS'S KNITTING TIPS

Oooh, my own knitting page! My advice on knitting a ... what is it? I know Mac told me, but I'm all of a fluster and me head's so full of nerves that I've plain forgot. Where's that bit of paper? Here we are ... ADVICE ON KNITTING A PLANE WING. Well I never. I've not done one of them before. I hope we've got enough wool.

But Mac's drawn it all out for us, look, and we just follow her pictures. So just knit one, and knit another one, and just keep knitting ... She's very clever, that Mac. Specially for a chicken.

And that Ginger, she's lovely. Keeps going off on holiday. I don't know where she finds the time to do that and all her escaping stuff. Really, I don't know what all the escaping fuss is about. As I say, if we'd been meant to fly, then we'd have been given wings. Ones that work proper, anyway.

Mind, I liked that Rocky. He was lovely. He's gone off on holiday too. I hope he took the beak-warmer I knitted him. There's nothing worse than getting a cold in your beak. Apart from being chopped up and made into a pie, of course. That's worse.

Knit and knit and knit some more. How are we going? Where's that note Mac gave us? It's where, Thora? Oh, don't worry about it, I'm sure it wasn't as important as you blocking that draught in the window.

Knit and knit and ... are we done? Let's have a look at it. A beautiful woollen scarf for Mac. Except - ooh dear. Thora, run and get that bit of paper, there's a love. I think I may have got a bit carried away.

7 a.m.	Wake up. Lay egg (traded for pair of pliers).
8 a.m.	Breakfast (chicken-feed).
8.43 a.m.	Lay egg (traded for bag of nails).
9 a.m.	Take stroll around chicken-run and find cricket ball.
11.15 a.m.	Manufacturing Committee asks for help with holding tail of flying machine so they can fix it on.
11.20 a.m.	Hold up tail of flying machine.
11.40 a.m.	Still holding up tail.
11.45 a.m.	Someone from Security Squad comes and asks why the tail is in view of the farmer and dogs. Explain problem. Security Squad goes off. Does not come back. Useless lot.
11.50 a.m.	Lay egg by accident.
11.52 a.m.	Realize Manufacturing Committee has gone to have a sit-down and a gossip.
11.53 a.m.	Throw cricket ball at Manufacturing Committee.
11.55 a.m.	Manufacturing Committee comes back, says sorry and finishes fixing the tail.
1.00 p.m.	Lunch.
1.30 p.m.	After-lunch snooze.
3.00 p.m.	Wake up. Find I've laid two eggs.
3.20 p.m.	Go and see Mac, who wants me to try a pedalling thing.
3.22 p.m.	Pedal.
3.50 p.m.	Still pedalling.
3.51 p.m.	Pedalling thing breaks.
4.10 p.m.	Panic! Manufacturing Committee says it needs twelve balls of wool and right now. Nick and Fetcher say they'll give a discount for bulk, but still want an egg for every two balls.
4.15 p.m.	Back to the hut. Sit on perch. And p-u-s-s-h-h-h.
4.35 p.m.	One egg.
5.30 p.m.	Another egg. Feeling really tired and my behind feels like it's on fire. But if we don't get the wool then we'll all feel that way – in the oven!
7.20 p.m.	Done it!
7.30 p.m.	Eggs delivered, wool collected, everyone happy. I'm exhausted. Having a hard time getting comfortable on my perch, there's something hard and round in here ... I haven't laid another one without noticing it, have I? No, it's the cricket ball. Throw it out of the window. I think it hit that good-for-nothing Ducky from the Security Squad.

Bunty's
EGG-LAYING
Schedule

ROCKY'S GUIDE TO LIFE

Part Three: On the Road

So you've headed out on your own? I ain't gonna ask why because it ain't none of my business, and the ol' Rockster's had to make a swift get-away a few times himself, so he knows how you feel. So here's Rocky's guide to hitting the road without the road hitting back. There's three things you gotta remember:

EATING Life on the road ain't like life in the farmyard. Mealtimes ain't exactly regular and there's plenty of fellow travellers that'd like to see you as the main course. But when it comes to fillin' your own face, try any of these:
● Grass. Not very filling, but there's plenty of it.
● Nuts, berries and seeds. Great — as long as it's autumn.
● Bugs and worms. Let's just say this stuff is an acquired taste. But Mac said they were full of crunchy goodness (not worms — that's squidgy goodness).
● Rubbish. You'd be amazed how much food humans throw away. But most of it's disgusting, so this is last resortsville. (What is this cheese stuff anyway? It tastes like rotten milk.)

NOT GETTING EATEN You're a chicken, right? You look like a chicken, you smell like a chicken, and I gotta tell you, there's a pretty strong chance you taste like chicken too. So unless you wanna disguise yourself as a ferocious hawk or somethin' (an' good luck to ya), then stay out of the way of people, dogs, foxes, cats, trucks, other people, other chickens ... look, safest to just keep yourself to yourself. I mean, you didn't hit the road for the company, right? So avoid it. All of it.

MOVING ON And you gotta remember not to stay in one place. Otherwise you start gettin' attached to things and that ain't the life of a bird on the road. You're a migratory bird now - so don't worry about what you've left behind. Just keep your beak pointing down the road, keep looking ahead, not back ... hey, what is that over there? A billboard?

Hey ... look, pal, just ignore everthing I've taught you. Everything. I'm turning round. Some times a chicken's gotta do what a chicken's gotta do. I'm not sure what it is yet, but I' gonna find out. Ginger, here I co

Flying Machine
Production Timetable

What	Who	Status
Blueprints	Mac	All done, hen. And if this doesn't fly, then I'll eat my scarf. *Mac, if this doesn't fly, someone's going to eat all of us!*
Wings	Babs	Done
Flapping mechanism	Mac	Done but not tested – needs a day, maybe two.
Main body	Babs	Done – well, apart from a hole or two here and there.
Pedal-power system	Mac	Done and tested. It failed the test. But ne' fear, I'm on the case.
Undercarriage	Mac	Done but not tested – needs two days.
Cockpit	Fowler	All ship-shape. Ooh, are we making a ship now?
Life jackets	Babs	I need one more ball of wool and then I'll have finished the lot. **Wool?**
Pilot's parachute	Babs	Half done. Finished tomorrow.
Seats	Babs	Done
Seat covers	Babs	Not started yet. Two days? I was thinking of a nice pink colour.
Structural checks	Mac	I think Babs should finish the structure before we start these. And they'll take a week at least.
In-flight entertainment	Fowler	I was thinking of giving a talk on military discipline and the … **NO!**
Black box	Mac	There's no black box on the plans – what's it for? My lunch, of course.
Eggs so far	Bunty	/// /// //// //// //// //// ////

EMERGENCY!

The pie machine is working! We've had to ambush Mr Tweedy. Anything not finished yet, you've got five minutes! And everybody get into the machine NOW, because we're FLYING TONIGHT!

SAFETY CARD

Nick & Fetcher's Airline

Welcome aboard this Chicken Air flight from Tweedy's Farm to somewhere a long way away, or possibly into a smashed heap of firewood at the bottom of the fence.
For your safety, please read this card carefully.

BEFORE TAKE-OFF:

● Stow all hand-luggage on the ground outside the aircraft. We can't take anything with us. It'd weigh too much.

● Place your feet on the two pedals in front of you.

● Pedal your giblets out.

Please notice the following safety features of this aircraft:

● There aren't any. They'd weigh too much.

IN THE EVENT OF AN EMERGENCY:

● Try not to panic.

● Note the position of the emergency exits. There aren't any right now, but if things go wrong then Bunty will smash a hole through the side of the aircraft. Go through the hole.

● If the aircraft makes an emergency landing on solid ground then ... well, just hope that we didn't get up very high before we came down. Otherwise we're in trouble.

● If the aircraft makes an emergency landing on water then there is a life-jacket under your seat. Unfortunately it's been knitted, so it'll sink faster than you will.

● If the aircraft falls to bits in mid-flight then ... well, try the flapping stuff that Rocky taught us. You never know. It might help and it can't hurt. Unlike the landing, which probably will.

FLIGHT LOG of the FLYING MACHINE

Filed by: Wing Commander T. I. 'Buffy' Fowler
Flight number: 0001 and only
Mission briefing: Get the blinkin' thing into the air and over the fence. After that, who knows?

Time	Action
Zero hour – 60 secs	Instrument check. They're all there, as far as I can tell. No idea if any of them work. Still, I'll find out soon enough.
Zero hour	Chocks away! Scramble! Scramble! Full throttle! Pedal, ladies, pedal!
Zero +19 secs	Enemy artillery opens fire. I'd expected flak, but – Great Scott, we've been hit! Lost our nose-cone! This could affect our aerodynamic performance. (Hm. 'Aerodynamic performance'. I've been spending too much time with Mac.) Anyway, evasive manoeuvres! Hard left! Increase speed! Full throttle!
Zero +31 secs	Pull back on the stick and ease her up ... Good heavens! It worked! We're in the air! We're FLYING!
Zero +62 secs	Sudden loss of power. Shout at silly hens to keep pedalling. Power resumed.
Zero +77 secs	More anti-aircraft fire! By Jove, there's a bandit on our tail. Commence aerial bombardment – chuck bombs at the car's aerial! Payload loaded and eggs away! Direct hit! And suddenly, for the first time, I understand what 'Scramble!' means.
Zero +99 secs	Who put these trees here?
Zero +117 secs	Who put that giant Mrs Tweedy there? Aargh! Dive! Dive! (Steady, Fowler, you're sounding like one of those submarine fellows.)
Zero +131 secs	We've been hit! Prepare to repel boarders, prepa – there's a Yank in this plane! A civilian too! Get him out of here! He's never flown a plane before in his life! (Come to think of it, neither have I – but I'm not going to tell him that.) This would never have happened in my RAF days! Get out, sir! Shoo!
Zero +144 secs	The old crate's breaking up. Bail out! Where's my parachute? What's this? A knitted cockpit-cosy? That's no good! No other choice – I'm going to have to jump for it and FLAAA

AA AA AAP!

Wing Commander Fowler's
Observations on the Mission

They say any landing you can walk away from is a good one. I couldn't exactly walk away from landing upside-down in a hawthorn bush, but I think the mission can be judged a success. Not as smooth as one of Jocko's, back in my old RAF days, but I think the service would have been proud of me. And I rather enjoyed it. No chance to test the landing gear though. I say, I wonder if I could persuade Mac to design another one, so we can give it a proper workout. see what the old bird can do ...

DEFENDERS OF THE CROWN No 21   24   By Kind permission of the Min...

Daily Dales Reporter

.   No. 1162   Price: Tuppence ha'penny

UNIDENTIFIED FLYING THING SIGHTED

Enormous craft 'nothing to do with us' say RAF

There is speculation and panic in the Dales this morning after a giant object was seen flying low over the area last night. The thing was first spotted over Tweedy's Farm at about 11.20 p.m. by Thomas Fogginton, landlord of the Dog and Trousers.

It went through a series of dizzying aerobatic manoeuvres before disappearing somewhere near the Dale-Top Bird Sanctuary.

Secret Project

One witness, who wished to remain anonymous because she didn't want her neighbours to think she'd been drinking, said, 'Ooh, it was terrifying. It looked like an enormous chicken, like some dreadful messenger from the heavens. I swear I'll never bake another of my chicken pies, which have previously won so many awards at the annual show.'

This reporter contacted the RAF, who issued an official statement saying that they had nothing to do with any giant winged object in the Dales area last night. However, their spokesman would not deny that the Air Force might be working on secret projects involving giant chicken-shaped aircraft, possibly to fool enemy radar.

From Another World

Several people have wondered if the strange-shaped object could be connected to the recent sightings in the USA of giant flying craft, which are thought to come from other worlds, although they are supposed to be round, like saucers or pie-dishes, or long and thin like sausages. Three people in the area have reported finding strange lumps of a sticky brown substance in their gardens this morning. 'It smelled like gravy,' said one, 'but felt like uncooked pastry. I've no idea what it was.' Perhaps it may have been some kind of strange message from the unknown craft or perhaps the whole thing is just pie-in-the-sky.

The true nature of the giant flying object remains a mystery. In fact, at this time, the only thing known for sure is that it wasn't a giant flying chicken – because, of course, there's no such thing.

On other pages: Search for litter-lout stretches into third week, p.3. This week's recipe: Beef in Wellington Boots, p.7. Your stars: Vera Lynn and George Formby, p.9. Obituary: Bubbles the Goldfish, dead aged 3, p.10. Adverts for fertilizer and second-hand cars, p.11-27.

TWEEDYS GO WEEDY

In a shock move, Tweedys Farm has been put up for sale and the owners, Mr and Mrs Tweedy, are reported to be planning to move to the north of Scotland, where they hope to set up a seaweed farm.

'There's good money in seaweed,' said Mrs Melisha Tweedy, 'and the change will do us good. Scotland is lovely: it's a long way from anyone we might owe money to, and then there's the lack of chickens.'

'I told you they was organized,' added Mr Tweedy.

When asked why they decided to move so suddenly or what had happened to their plan to get rich by selling chicken pies, Mrs Tweedy turned an interesting shade of green and would not say any more. Mr Tweedy would only repeat, 'I told you they was organized,' but would not say who 'they' were.

There are understood to be no bidders for the farm at present.

Dear Diary,

I still can't believe it happened. You plan something for so long and then it all happens so fast that the only thing you can remember is the planning, not the doing.

But it worked! The Flying Machine flew — Fowler did an amazing job as pilot, the girls gave us all the power we needed, and even the rats did their bit, giving up their hard-earned eggs. And Rocky saved the day! That moment, when he rode into the farmyard on his tricycle, he looked so heroic that I forgave him everything.

It's taking me a while to get used to the idea of freedom. Rocky talked so much about life on the road and how good it was — well, there aren't any roads through here, but it's true that the grass really is greener.

Everyone's having a great time. The moment we got Fowler out of the hawthorn bush he'd landed in, he was striding about muttering things about 'marvellous turf', and he's already got a cricket team organized. Babs is knitting like crazy, making ground-sheets and blankets. She's even found a friendly sheep to supply her with wool. Bunty's at a bit of a loss now she doesn't have to spend all day laying eggs, but she's started looking after our security ... and after she beat up two local foxes and a whole pack of weasels, they've agreed to leave us alone.

And Rocky ... he's great. Doing really well. Not doing very much really. He's all right when you get to know him. I've heard the others calling us 'love-birds', but I think they're just jealous.

The one I'm worried about is Mac. She's still spending all day pouring over plans for some new invention, muttering about 'power boosters', 'throost co-efficients' and Wensleydale'. I caught her gazing up at the moon last night and when I asked her why, she just smiled, pointed up into the sky and said, 'Escape velocity'. But we've already escaped! Whatever is she planning now?

Ginger

What did you make of it? It's an important document you are holding. Actual stuff put together by the very chickens involved in the very 'Chicken Run' escape. Soon to be a major motion picture! An' I 'ear tell that they might be gettin' Jimmy Cagney to play me. You know. 'You dirty rat - oo, you dirty rat.'

Nick, it _is_ a major motion picture, that's the 'ole point. Anyway, we went through a lot to get all this stuff and it's got huge sentimental value for us. So, how many sentiments would you pay for it, then?

I don't think we should sell it. It's got our business plan in, right? Starting a chicken farm of our own? So all we need is the book and a chicken ...

Naw, an egg, 'cos an egg will hatch into a chicken ...

Naw a chicken 'cos the chicken lays an egg.

You need to start with an egg because you can't count your chickens before they're hatched.

No, a chicken because an egg can't cross a road on its own ...

Egg! Chicken! Egg! Chicken! Egg!

THE END